Emmanuel Guibert

Marc Boutavant

ARIOL

Happy as a Pig...

PAPERCUTZ™

Happy as a Pig...

To Mrs. Nays,
– Emmanuel Guibert

ARiOL

#3 Happy as a Pig...

Emmanuel Guibert – Writer
Marc Boutavant – Artist
Rémi Chaurand – Colorist
Joe Johnson – Translation
Michael Petranek – Lettering
Beth Scorzato – Production Coordinator
Michael Petranek – Associate Editor
Jim Salicrup
Editor-in-Chief

ISBN: 978-1-59707-487-2

Printed in China
December 2013 by New Era Printing, LTD.
Unit C. 8/F Worldwide Centre
123 Chung Tau, Kowloon
Hong Kong

Papercutz books may be purchased for business or promotional use. For information on bulk purchases please contact Macmillan Corporate and Premium Sales Department at (800) 221-7945 x5442.

Distributed by Macmillan
First Papercutz Printing

ARIOL
After School
Why do you always want to walk me home after school?
Because I love you.
Uh... Well...

I can get home by myself. I don't need anybody to come with me.

Yes, no, I know. But it's just to-- uh... like this, that's what. To talk.

No, it's because I love you.

It's terrible.
I've got nothing
to say to her.

Oh, yeah, that's it! That's not bad.
You know, I'm walking
with you to protect you.
To protect me?

If someone bothers you, I'll defend you.
And how will you
defend me?

My dad can defend me because he's a
big, really strong bull with huge muscles
and pointy horns. You-- you're little,
you don't even have horns and, what's
more, you have glasses.

Well? How would you defend me?
Listen, PETULA, if someone bothers you, I'll kill him, that's all. Even a dinosaur.

HAHAHA! You're really super brave!
I'm not super brave, but I don't want anybody bothering you.

Hold out your arm.
What, my arm?

I'm going to pinch your arm to see if you're brave.
OH? Okay.

Am I dreaming? She's pinching my arm.

It's wonderful.

I hope she leaves a mark.
Okay, I'll stop.

All right, you're brave. You can protect me, but just for today. For the other days, I'll make you take more tests.
No problem.

Walk behind me, please.
Huh? Why behind you?

Well, to protect me. In front, I see what's happening, I don't need someone to protect me. You protect someone from behind.
Really.

Yes, but it's not easy for talking to each other.
You've got nothing to say anyhow.

That's true.

But whenever I'm in class, behind her, I can't stop talking to her in my head. And once I get to talk to her for real, POW! my mind goes blank.

I need some little danger now, so I can protect her. Some danger that's not dangerous.
Okay, ARIOL...

I made it home. Goodbye.
Uh... you want me to protect you in the elevator?
No. Don't bother.

SEE YOU TOMORROW, EH?
CLAC

SIGH

Hey, PETULA?

Give me your backpack. I'll carry it for you.

There. Will you let me put my arm around your neck?

It's better like this, isn't it? Hey, I'm going to ask you a riddle.

Do you know how you get four elephants into a small car?

No? You don't know?

Well, it's simple: two in front and two in back. HAHAHAHA!

Yes, I love you, too.

END

ARiOL
The Submarines
UNDERGROUND PARKING
How about we go down into the basement?
Are you crazy?

We said we're going to play soccer with our friends at the big field.
We'll go later. First, let's go to the basement.

I want to see what your basement is like.
It's ugly, dirty, dark, and cold. That's what it's like.

You afraid?
No, I'm not afraid. But it's dangerous. We could get lockjaw.

What's lockjaw?
It's a fatal illness, and afterwards, you stay handicapped.

My dad's always holed up in his basement and he's never gotten anything.
Except for bottles of wine, HAHAHA!

Okay, so you've seen the basement? Can we go back up?
Wait, there's no hurry! We can play for two minutes!

With all these pipes here, it's like we're in a submarine movie.
Okay, I'm heading up. Later.

CRRR... TOOWEET! ALERT! CRRR... ENEMY APPROACHING... ARM THE TORPEDOS!
RAMONO! Stop!

⇒KKFRRRSCHH!⇐ WE'VE BEEN HIT! THERE'S A WATER LEAK! ⇒PCHHHHH!⇐
Surface, if there's a leak!

?
?

ARIOL, did you turn the light off?
Uh... no.

It's all dark, like in a submarine movie.
We've got to find the stairs.

Normally, in submarine movies, there's a little, green light that comes on just after the explosion.
You're annoying me with your submarine movie. We're not in a submarine, we're in a dirty basement and we're going to catch lockjaw! All because of you!

EXIT
Hey, just like I said! The little, green light!
Going there's against the rules. It's the parking garage.

Wow! We've found the secret submarine base!
We can't go there because of the cars.

Okay, you stay alone in the dark, and I'll go to the submarine's secret base.
Uh... no. You need me. I'm coming, too.

Are you armed? I have an exoskeleton and a laser cannon.
Yeah. I have two of each of them.

LOOK OUT!
Huh? What?

Wh-- what did you see?
Enemies.

I'll circle around them this way, and you circle around them that way.
No. Let's stay together, that's better.

Okay. But first I'm peeing. I've got to.
Don't pee on Mrs. CAPRA's car! She's the neighbor who looks after me when my parents aren't home!
BGCQ21X

So what?
So, she's nice. Let's pee on Mr. GREENWAY's car.
BGCQ21X

Mr. GREENWAY's dumb.
Well, we'll sink his atomic submarine with our laser cannons!

BRODOBRODO BROM!
AAAH!

BRODOBRODOBRODOBR
Are they shooting at our backs?
No, it's the garage door opening.

Let's hide! If it's my dad coming back, he's going to chew us out!
Wait, I'm almost done.

Whew! It's not my dad! It's Miss MISTY.
And what if we used the door being opened to escape the secret base?

Then we run, because the door will shut by itself.
Wait, I'm zipping up.

BRODOBRODOBRODOBR
Hurry up, RAMONO! You'll be stuck.
Coming! Stick your foot in the door!

CLACK
OOF!

That was close.
Mission accomplished.
SLAP
SLAP

Aw darn! The ball...

END

ARiOL
MRS. CAPRA
DINNERTIME, ARIOL!
They're calling you.
I know, I heard.
SOK!
POW
THUNDER HORSE
TRILOGY
CHEWS

You don't want to stay for dinner with me?
No, I have to go home. I promised my mom.
POW
CLACK

Come on, be nice, stay! That way, we have dinner, and afterwards, we'll play more.
No.
POP
BOOM

You're dumb! We were having fun!
You're the one who's dumb! You're going to eat carrots, and I'm going to have a truffle omelet.
BING
PEF

You're still roughhousing, boys! Dinner time, ARIOL! The carrots are cooked.
Just having fun, Mrs. CAPRA.
I'm leaving, Mrs. CAPRA.

Will you loan me your VIDEOGAME? I'll give it back tomorrow.
Okay.
Thanks.

And a comicbook? Can I grab a comicbook?
If you want. Here, take this one, it's not bad.

"SARDINE IN OUTER SPACE." Is there fighting?
Tons.

Because I like fighting!
KAPOW!
KAPOW! Missed!
WHIF

THUNDER HORSE...
AVENGER OF THE STARS...
POKE
WHAK

ARIOL, you come, now! And you get home, RAMONO! Your mom will be worried.
Coming, Mrs. CAPRA.
I'm going, Mrs. CAPRA.

Okay, so, see you tomorrow then.
See you tomorrow at eight-thirty.

You're nothing but a dirty, limp sausage, because I'm loaning you my game and my comicbook, and you ditch me.

I'm ditching you because you're an old carrot-eater, with 95 mile-long ears.

Oh, yeah?
Yeah.

THUNDER HORSE...
TRAVELER TO THE STARS...
BAF
CRUNCH

Okay, enough with THUNDER HORSE!
Bye, RAMONO!
LATER, ARIOL! Goodbye, MRS. CAPRA!

Are Mrs. CAPRA's creamed carrots good?
They're good, but you make them too often.

Do you know about truffles?
Of course I know about truffles.

RAMONO's mom makes him a truffle omelet. It's really good.
It's super expensive, too.

RAMONO's mom makes him a truffle omelet, because her uncle lives in the country and sends her truffles, you understand?
If you buy them in town, they're awfully expensive.

Ask RAMONO to give you some, and I'll make you a truffle omelet.
RAMONO's good for taking, but not very much for giving.

But he's your best friend.
Oh, yeah, other than that, he's cool.

And explain to me a little why you are CONSTANTLY roughhousing with each other?
We're not fighting, we're having fun.

I can see you're having fun, but there are other ways to have fun, aren't there?
It's because we're playing THUNDER HORSE.

THUNDERHORSE! Always THUNDERHORSE!
It's cool!

When I'm big, I'll get my ears redone to look like THUNDER HORSE!
ARIOL, I forbid you to say such rubbish.

Mom and Dad are okay with it!
Your dad and mom made you like this, we love you like this, you stay like this!

Moreover, your little ears are adorable. They suit you very well.
I've had enough carrots.

LATER...
One game apiece! Rubber match, Mrs. CAPRA?
It's nine-twenty, ARIOL. You should already be in bed.

Especially since we still have to get you washed up and brush your teeth.
You're saying that because you're afraid of losing.

When does Mom get back?
Late. They said around eleven o'clock. She'll come kiss you goodnight in your bed, even if you're asleep.

Are you going to watch TV?
Well, yes, with my knitting.

Turn to channel four. There's a good movie on.
Okay, goodnight, ARIOL. Sleep tight and sweet dreams.

END

ARiOL
Poetry
Mom, I'm fed up.
What now?

I have to learn a poem by heart, and I can't.
Show me.

Okay, come on! It's not long!
Yes, it's long. It has eleven lines, plus the title and the author's name.

And anyhow, I don't like poetry. It's stupid and it's useless.
You're wrong. Poetry's very beautiful.

What's more, it's not true it's useless. Without poetry, maybe you wouldn't be here.
Really? Why not?

When I met your father, he wrote me very pretty poems. It's partly for that that I fell in love with him and you were born.
No joke?

And can I read them?
Ah, no, that's secret. What's more, I've completely forgotten where I put them.

So, if you write poems to girls, they fall in love?
It can help.

Hey, Dad! Is it true you wrote poems to Mom?
Uh-- yes. Not recently, but--

What did they talk about?
Ah, well, they were poems to make her happy. I'd tell her that she was beautiful.

But I'd write that it in a poetic style, with comparisons. For example, instead of just writing: "you have pretty ears..."

I'd write: "Your ears are as soft as velvet."
What's velvet?
A very soft fabric.

And what else would you write her?
I forget. Let me watch the news now.

SHORTLY...
PETULA, your ears are soft like velvet (a very soft fabric). Your hair--

Your hair--
Your hair--

Hair's not easy. I'll put that off and do that later.

Your eyes are pretty like two TV's showing cartoons all the time.
That's not bad.

Your voice is so beautiful that, when you grow up, you'll surely do the intercom announcements in airports or supermarkets.

Mom?
Yes?
Is it spelled "ariport" or "airport"?
AIRport.

A-I-R-Ports.

It's true that poetry is beautiful.

THE NEXT DAY...
PETULA isn't here?
No, she has a sore throat.

Darn it! And I wanted to slip my poem into her backpack!
Who wants to recite? ARIOL?

Uh-- I didn't learn the poem, sir.
Really? Why not?

Because, in fact, I wrote one.
Well, well! That's not what I asked for, but that's interesting.

Go on, read us your poem.
Oh, no! It's not a poem for you.
Ha ha!
Ha ha ha!

Well, since you like writing poetry, ARIOL, you can write this for me fifty times: "I must never shirk, Doing my homework."
Oh, no, sir!

AT RECESS...
How's it going?
Leave me be, BIZZBILLA. I'm doing my punishment.

You want me to help you?
Well, no, it has to all be in my handwriting.

Okay then, I'll leave you alone.
Yes. Leave me alone.

Ariol,
I think it's really
beautiful that you write
poems,
and although

Mister Blunt
gives you lines
to write or problems
I love you even so.
Bizzbilla

END

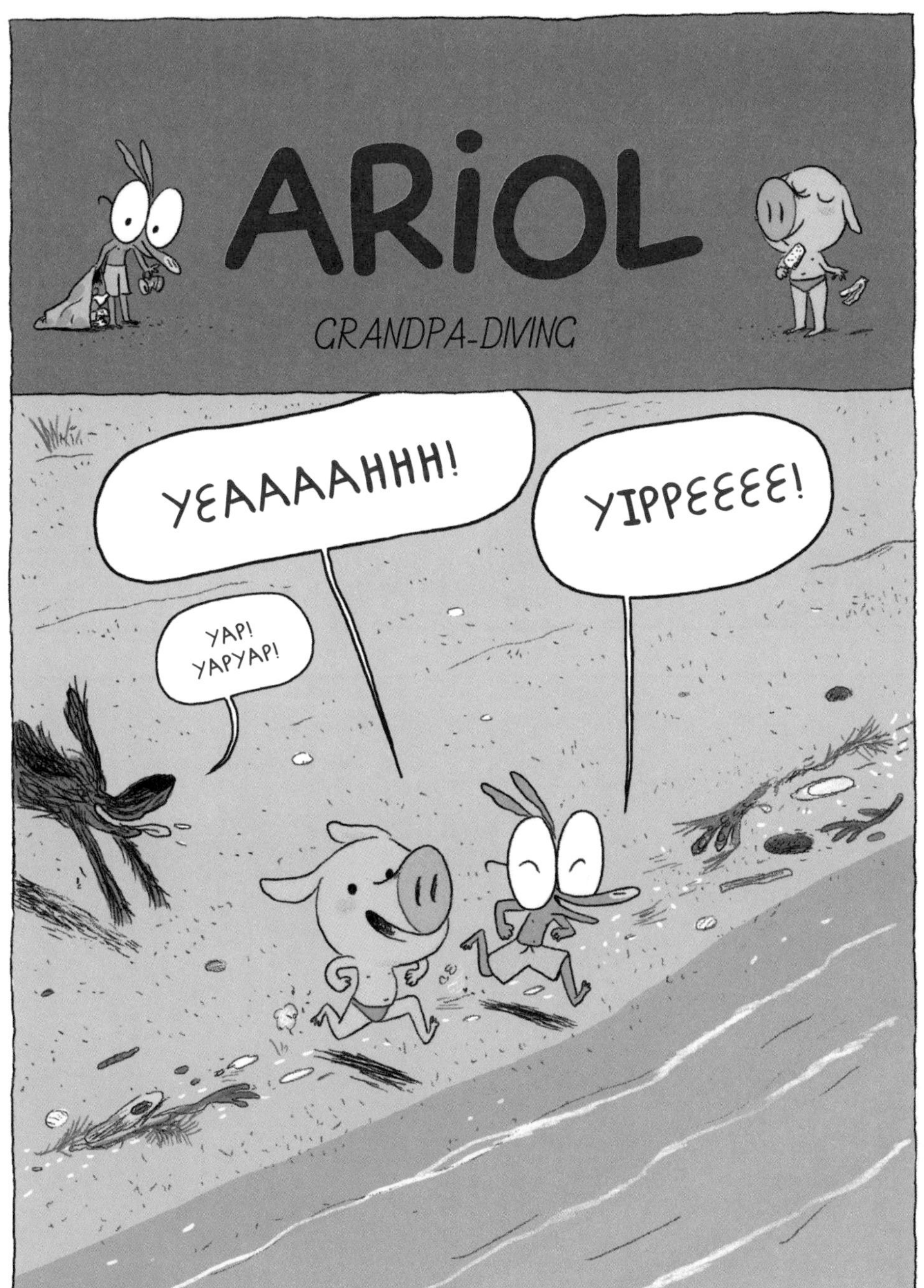
ARiOL
GRANDPA-DIVING
YAP! YAPYAP!
YEAAAAHHH!
YIPPEEEE!

WHOA!
WHOA!
Yap!
Yap!
Yikes, it's cold!
BRRRRR!
SPLISH
SPLISH
SPLISH

Yap!
SPLASH
SPLASH
SPLASH

Your dog sucks!
Hahaha!

That makes you laugh?
No! Don't splash me!
SPLASH
SPLASH
Arf?

TIME OUT! TIME OUT!
I have my glasses on!
So what?

So, I forgot to take them off
and seawater damages them!
Whatever!

Grandpa, can you keep
my glasses?
Put them in
the basket,
cabin boy!

And here, take these, if you like.
They're diving goggles Grandpa
bought for you and your buddy.
WOW! SUPER!
Thanks, Grandpa!

Hey! RAMONO! Look what I have!
What?

Goggles for going underwater.
Will you loan 'em to me?
No.

Loan 'em, or I'll splash you.
I'm not loaning them to you, I'm giving them to you. There's a pair for you. It's a gift from my grandpa.
Go on, show me.

So, pirates? Happy with your goggles?
Oh, yes, Grandpa!
It'd be cool to have flippers, too.

Go on, you bandits! Into the water! Do like me: first you wet your arms...
The goggles squeeze your head and everything looks yellow.

Then your torso and your neck...
Yeah, you know, you're right. They hurt.

I'm taking them off.
Wait, I'm gonna look under the water a little, even so.
...And go!
SHOPLOSH

AAAH! That's better!

So? What did you see?
Well, nothing. Some sand.

We'll ask Grandpa to return the goggles and get us some flippers instead.
Or an inflatable raft.
Or some ice cream.
Or buy us movie tickets.

Grandpa! We don't want the goggles! We left them on the beach.
That's fine. I'm glad you like them.

Your grandpa's deaf.
No way. He just has water in his ears.
Come on! We're going to play GRANDPA-DIVING!

We played it last year!
Here, climb on my back,
we'll show ROMANO.
RA MO NO!
Psst Psst
Heeheehee
Psst--

Are you there, ARIOL? Ready?
YES!
Heehee!
Well, go ahead,
jump. And don't
forget to shout...

GRANDPA-DIVE!
YA-HOOOO!
ARF!

YAP YAP
YAP!
KER
SPLOOSH

What are you doing here, REX? What do you have in your mouth?
Give.
Arfl Glorpf

Ah, well now! Diving goggles just like yours, kids! Where'd you steal them from, REX?
But those are ours, GRANDPA!
YAP! YAP!

Play nice, you buccaneers. Grandpa's going to take these goggles back to their owners.
BUT WE'RE TELLING YOU THEY'RE OURS!
Forget it, ARIOL.

Your grandpa's deaf.
Well, yeah. A little. But did you see how strong he is?

Want to go get the ball?
Yeah. First one to it!

SPLISH SPLISH SPLASH

HEY! I got it!
BAH! Only 'cause it's really hard running on sand!

It's good, eh?

Not bad. Look: I dropped a piece, and there are lots of ants on it. And I'm burying them under the sand.

END

ARIOL
The Book-Signing
NOUVEL ALBUM!
THE ARTIST GIDDY IS SIGNING COPIES OF THUNDER HORSE'S FAMOUS ADVENTURES AT THE BOOTH FOR CHAURAND EDITIONS.
Faster, Daddy, faster!
ARIOL, don't pull on my jacket!
SKULL
CHIBOUZ
DUGE
Thunder Horse
OUAH
miceman

Where's the THUNDER HORSE booth?
How should I know? We have to ask.
Thunder Horse

Excuse me, sir, where's the THUNDER HORSE booth, please?
In back.
Thunder Horse

In back! He's a funny one! In back where?
Ah, I see it! It's back there!
Thunder Horse

ARIOL, I forbid you to leave me! Or else we'll lose each other!
Don't pull on my tee-shirt!

Great! The line's five miles long!

I have an idea.

It's terrible, these kids want everything right away!
Mine are the same. No patience.
Thunder Horse

My dad's dumb!
Ours is, too.

We're CHANG HI and CHANG LOW.
We're twins.
My name's ARIOL. An only child.

Do you see, CHANG LOW? Our two dads are talking amongst themselves.
Yes, CHANG HI. Let's take this chance to get away. Are you coming, ARIOL?
Uh-- well--

Hey! But, guys, where are you going? We're not going to watch GIDDY drawing?
We don't care about GIDDY!

We don't like comicbooks.
It's our dad who collects them.
He makes us stand in line for hours.
All for a stupid, little drawing!

Video games are what we like.
What's more, the THUNDER HORSE video game is a lot better than the comicbook. Do you know it?

I can't go too far away. My dad will worry.
BAH! Just ten minutes!
Our dad's super talkative. He'll wear your dad out. They won't even realize we've left!

Hey, look. There are tons of video games on display here.
WOW! Did you see that, CHANG HI?
TYPE YOUR NAME

MOOK WARRIOR III is out! I can't believe it!
Want to play, CHANG LOW?
Hey--

Here we go, CHANG HI! Do you see the backgrounds?
Top class, CHANG LOW!
Hey, guys--

Take me back to my dad!
You drive, and I'll shoot, CHANG LOW.
Watch out for the big, hairy monster on the left, CHANG HI.
Do you hear me?

They're not even listening to me! I'll have to go back without them.
TATATATATATATA
HAHA! I got you, CHANG LOW.

Which way do I go? It's jammed with people, and everything looks the same. What's more, I'm too shy to ask anyone.

OOOOH... I'm lost! This makes me want to cry and poop in my pants.

AH, BUT, NO! I RECOGNIZE THAT! IT'S THAT WAY!

Uh-oh, Dad's not in line anymore!

Sir, sir? Where's my father?
There you are! Where are my boys?
GIDDY
Thunder Horse

It's your turn, sir.
Ah, yes. Hello, Mr. GIDDY. Here, if you could draw me a little THUNDER HORSE.
GIDDY

There. And to whom?
Put: For--
ARIOL!
GIDDY

YOU STUPID DONKEY! Where'd you go? You really scared me!
It wasn't me, Dad. It was the twins.

I'D TOLD YOU TO NOT BUDGE FROM HERE! YOU DISOBEYED ME! Because of that, you won't get a signed copy!
OH, OKAY, DAD!

Ah, but, no, Mister GIDDY! You're mistaken! You wrote down: For ARIOL. My name's not ARIOL!
Ah, I don't know. That's what you said to me.
GIDDY

But, no, I never said that! It's very annoying! I'm a collector! I don't want a copy which doesn't have my name!
Okay, give me another one, I'll sign you one again.
GIDDY

All right, come, ARIOL! Just be happy I don't take away your copy! And let that be a lesson to you!

Oh, yes, Dad!

END

ARiOL
AT RAMONO'S
Are you coming to watch THUNDER HORSE at my house?
No, are you crazy?
I won't be a bother?
31

Quick, RAMONO! It's going to start!
Wait, dang it! I can't find my key.

Ring the bell. Maybe my sister's there.
Ding dong

Is that you, doofus? You couldn't open with your key?
I don't know where it is.

Next time you'll stay outside!
Hi, PORKY.

CLIK
It's starting.
Just in time!

Thunder Horse...
THUNDER HOOOORSE...

AVENGER OF THE STARS...
AVENGER OF THE STAAAAAARRS...

TARARATA LATALA!

WHOA! Are you done shouting? I'm trying to call MOMO now!
THUNDER HORSE
Shut up, fatso!

RAMONO, you don't talk to me like that!
SPACE VOYAGER
Shut up, fatso!

Gimme that remote!
No!

I'll put some music on for you, you'll see!
GIVE IT BACK!
CLICK

I may be just a poor monkey
III MAYBE JUSTUH POOR MONKEEEEY
GIVE BACK THE REMOTE!

but I love you !
BUT I LUVYOOOO
DON'T MAKE ME HIT YOU!

BOOM
OWW!
CLICK

...CUT OFF BY PSCOPI ...PISCOPI PASSES TO HAZIB. LONG CLEARING SHOT ACROSS THE FIELD...
HAHAHA! Stop, you're tickling me!
GIVE IT BACK!

BALL RECOVERED BY ZAVANI... ZAVANI... ZAVANI STILL--
HEEHEEHEE HOOHOOHOO
ARiOL, CATCH!

FOUL! FOUL BY CHEPIF ON ZAVANI! IT'S A FREE KICK!
GO ON, CHANGE THE CHANNEL!
I can't, it's a telephone!

MY CELLPHONE!
BLABLABLABLABLABLABLABLAB
GIMME THE REMOTE!
HELP!

GIMME!
HELLO, MOMO? YOU HEAR ME? ARE YOU STILL THERE?
You're squashing me...
POW POW

WHAT'S ALL THIS MAYHEM?
IT'S PORKY, SHE WON'T GIMME BACK THE REMOTE!
Blah Blah Blah
HELLO, MOMO? WHERE'D YOU GO? HELLOHELLOHELLO?
Good evening, ma'am...

GIMME THAT REMOTE AND GO YOUR ROOM!
I'M CALLING MOMO BACK AND I'M TELLING HIM TO COME GET ME ON HIS SCOOTER!
SHUT UP!

CLIK
HEY! WHY'D YOU CHANGE THE CHANNEL?
It's time for my soap opera.

BUT WE WERE WATCHING--
QUIET! GO DO YOUR HOMEWORK! And take the slop pie out of the freezer, so it'll defrost!

That sucks! We missed THUNDER HORSE! I hope they'll repeat it on Sunday.

You're not talking? Are you mad?
No, it's PORKY. She crushed me with her chest and she twisted an earpiece of my glasses.

Show me? Oh, yeah.
Have you ever seen her chest?

Well, of course I've seen her chest! She's my sister!
What are they like?
Ugly. Huge. They go BOING BOIINNGGG!

You want a cookie?
Yeah. And then I'm going.

Anyhow, did you see? When you come here, you don't bother anybody!

Bye, RAMONO. See you tomorrow.

Hello, PORKY? It's MOMO. Yeah, I'm downstairs. You coming down?

END

ARiOL
The Light in the Hallway
THUNDER HORSE
MORODAN
PAN PAN
I ♥ NY
Sweet dreams, ARIOL.
You'll leave the light on in the hallway, with the door cracked open, okay?
Yes, don't worry.

Sleep well, honey.
Sleep well, Mom.
THUNDER HORSE

TATATA!
THUNDER HORSE

THUNDER HORSE comes out of his secret hiding place! It's nighttime, but he can see a little thanks to the moonlight in the hallway.
THUNDER HORSE

He advances, crawling over the desert squares. FRRRT FRRRT!
THUNDER HORSE

Suddenly, ⇒BUDDABOOM!⇐ There's a large mountain shooting up in the middle of the desert!
THUNDER HORSE

All of a sudden, THUNDER HORSE loses his balance and falls out of the bed,
"AAAAH!"
THUNDER HORSE

BUT, NO! At the last instant, he catches himself on the edge of the cliff with just his fingertips and he says: "A-ARIOL-- help me, I-I'm going to-- fall--"

And I say: "Don't worry, THUNDER HORSE, I'm here!" and I pull him back up on the bed!
And he says: "Thanks, ARIOL, you saved my life. You're my best friend!"

And then, THUNDER HORSE starts to climb the mountain, ⇒CLOP CLOP CLOP!⇐
THUNDER HORSE

What he doesn't know is that, on the other side of the mountain, TATATA!, his enemy is there, the EMPEROR MORODAN, who's hiding out.
THUNDER HORSE

And when THUNDER HORSE reaches the summit, the EMPEROR MORODAN leaps out and says: "HAHA! I WAS WAITING FOR YOU, THUNDER HORSE!"
THUNDER HORSE

AND POW! They start to battle one another
⇒BONG! BLAH! AAARG!⇐
THUNDER HORSE

But ZWITCH! THUNDER HORSE snares the EMPEROR MORODAN's legs with his magic lasso.
HAHA! I got you, MORODAN!
THUNDER HORSE

AND SWISH!
He flings him to the other end of the room!
CHAK

ARIOL, what's all this commotion?
It's nothing, Dad. I'm sleeping.
It's late, we don't want to hear you anymore.

What's more, if you're asleep, there's no point running the electricity for nothing. I'll turn off the light in the hallway.
OH, NO!
CLIK

TURN IT BACK ON!
QUIET!

MOM SAID I COULD HAVE THE LIGHT ON! THIS ISN'T FAIR! TURN IT BACK ON!

ARIOL, STOP YOUR BRAYING RIGHT NOW OR DADDY'S GOING TO PULL YOUR EARS! UNDERSTOOD?
Yes, yes.

Hey! I have a booger in my nose.

I'll stick it under the bed with the others.

It's funny, because the old boogers which are dry, crackle under your finger.

AAH! The light's back on!
Mercy...

Mercy, THUNDER HORSE, don't hurt me!
Well? It seems that you were hard on ARIOL, my best friend!

What do you want me to do to this wicked dad, ARIOL?
Oh, nothing.

You just have to pull on his ears a little.
Okay.
NOOOO! NOT MY EARS!

HELP ME!
Can I come in, ARIOL?
PETULA?
NOK NOK

Uh... no! Don't come in! I'm in my pajamas.
It's okay, I'm in my pajamas, too.

I came to see if you wanted me to go to sleep with you, in your bed.
Ah... but, uh... okay. Get in.

Your bedroom is big.
It's not my bedroom, it's the desert of squares.

And we're on the top of a big mountain and THUNDER HORSE is climbing up to join us.
CLOP, CLOP, CLOP.

Mission accomplished, ARIOL! THE EMPEROR MORODAN is defeated.
Super.

Sleep well, children. I'll watch over you.
May I give you a kiss?
Well, yeah, go ahead.

ZZZZZ

END

ARiOL
EXIT→
←EXIT
Granny in the Subway
ONE NIGHT ONLY
Say, Granny Annie...
Yes, my treasure?
How do you not get lost in the subway?
GREMLIN

Oh! It's because I've been taking the subway my whole life.
How do you know we have to turn here, for example?

Because it's the corridor leading to our line.
But how do you know?
It's marked, sweetie.

Look: GOAT BRIDGE.
We're going to GOAT BRIDGE?
No, GOAT BRIDGE is the direction.
8 DIRECTIONS →
GOAT BRIDGE

We're stopping at the GOATEBORG station.
Geez! I don't understand a thing!
DIRECTIONS →

Don't worry, come on! You can't get lost with your old granny!
Don't let go of me, okay?

Here you go.
Thanks, ma'am. Good evening.
I'm Hungry

That poor lady's been there for months. I give her change every time I come by.
You'd do better to show her the way out.

OOOH! LOOK, GRANNY!
What is it, my dear?

I can't believe it!
This man is selling posters of
THUNDER HORSE!
Cheap.
THUNDER HORSE

ARIOL, Granny will buy you a poster in
a real store. It's dirty here.
Cheap,
ma'am.
THUNDER HORSE

I've never seen these in stores.
Come on, Granny, buy them for me!
All three,
cheap.

Come on,
ARIOL!
All of them
cheap.
OH, Granny,
please!

Granny will buy you what you want, honey, but not those old rags lying on the ground.
They were really nice!

Oh, goodness me! With all this fuss, you've gotten me all turned around!
Well, come on, we'll go back to the poster salesman!
EXIT

RUMBLERUMBLERUMBLERUMBLERUMBLE
Granny? What's that noise?
Oh, no! It's rush hour!

RUMBLERUMBLERUMBLERUMBLE
Quick, sweetie! Let's take shelter in the hallway!

RUMBLERUMBLE

Who are all those people?
It's the herd of horned beasts leaving work and going home. We'd best stand aside.

Will it last long?
Well, the time it takes for the herd to pass.

What if we took that escalator?
No, I don't really know where it goes, up yonder.

Hey, look, Granny? Your handbag is going up all by itself.
MY BAG?!

Oh, no, oh, no, oh, no! I set my bag on the escalator!
I'll go get it!

ARIOL! STAY WITH GRANNY! WE'LL LOSE EACH OTHER!
I'll bring you back your bag!

Oh, god, oh, god, oh, god, protect that child!

ARIOL? WHERE ARE YOU?

HE'S DISAPPEARED!
HE'S BEEN KIDNAPPED!

HELP! THIEF! KIDNAPPER!

Are you looking for your grandson, ma'am?
HAVE YOU SEEN HIM?

He went running by, two minutes ago.
GOD BE PRAISED!
I'm Hungry

Granny ANNIE!
ARIOL! MY SUNSHINE!

Here, Granny! I found your bag!
You mustn't ever run off like that, sweetheart! I nearly died with worry!

It's because the bag had tumbled, uh-- towards the man who was selling the cheap posters. So, as a result, I bought some from him.
You'll drive me crazy!

Once you've located where the THUNDER HORSE posters are, you can't get lost.

I've had enough of the subway for one evening. Let's go out and take the bus.

EXIT

I'm Hungry

END

ARIOL
VOLCANS
DICO
Today, Reports.
BIZZBILLA, ARIOL, and RAMONO, we'll listen to your report on volcanoes. Who'll start?
Uh... me.

Go ahead, ARIOL. First, a definition. What's a volcano?
Well... it's a mountain that smokes.

Yes, if you like. But you'll have to be a little more precise. Why does it smoke?
Can I do a drawing on the board?

Good idea. Do your drawing.
So there. That's the volcano.

And on top, there's a hole.
What's that hole called?

Uh... the volcano hole?
The crater!

I can hear BIZBILLA's whispering it to you.
The crater?
Yes. Write that beside it.

And so then, the hole is very deep and it goes down to--
Wait. You made a big mistake.
CRATERRE

A mistake where?
T-E-R, not E-R-R-E!
CRATERRE

Instead of whispering, BIZZBILLA, correct it yourself. That'll teach him.
I can't. It's too high.
CRATERRE

RAMONO, then. Correct it.
Who's that?
CRATERRE

Give me the chalk, ARIOL.
CRATERRE

A CRATER. In effect, it's a basin on top of the volcano. And it's spelled like this.
CRATER

Okay, go on.
So, I was saying that the hole goes all the way to the center of the Earth, where there's fire.
CRATER

And so, the fire makes the smoke that goes up the hole and comes out on top. And the volcano smokes.
It smokes like what?
CRATER
Like my sister.

What are you saying, RAMONO?
Nothing.
It smokes like a CHIMNEY.
CRATER

Good job, BIZZBILLA. The CONDUIT or central pipe that ARIOL has drawn is like a CHIMNEY. Write that, ARIOL.
Yes.

Now, I'll turn the talk over to RAMONO, who's going to talk to you about the fire under the Earth.
Already?
CRATER
CHIMNEY
HaHa

Uh... hello... As ARIOL said, in the middle of the Earth, there's fire--
What's this fire like?
Very hot!
CHIMNEY

Yes, okay, but what is it similar to? And what is it called?
It's very, very hot. And what's more, just talking about is making me hot. So I'm going to take off my sweater.
CHIMNEY

Pssst! BIZBILLA! What's the fire called?
MAGMA.
CRATER
CHIMNEY

AAAH! That's better! Well, this fire is called MAGMA. And you mustn't touch it, or else you'll get burned!
CRATER
CHIMNEY

And now, I'll pass the mike to BIZZBILLA, who's going to talk to you about irruptions.
E-ruptions, RAMONO. Your report was done pretty fast! Write MAGMA on the board then.

Right away. But before that, I'll put my sweater back on because I'm a little cold now.
Pssst! BIZZBILLA! How do you spell MAGMA?
M-A-G-M-A.

My turn. I'm going to talk to you about eruptions. A volcano is simple, in fact. It's like a person who has a huge secret she can't say.
CRATER
CHIMNEY

Your example is bizarre, BIZBILLA.
No, no. You'll see that I'm right.
CRATER
CHIMNEY
MAJMA

This person has a huge, burning secret hidden in her heart, like the fire under the Earth, but it can't be seen from outside, because she doesn't say anything.
CRATER
CHIMNEY
MAJMA

And then one day, the secret gets so big it goes up her throat and
BOOM!
CRATER
Haha!
Hoohoohoo
Heehee
Blablabla
Heheheh
Hoho!
Pssst!
Pssst

Quiet, class! Let her finish!
BOOM!
The person explodes and tells HER HUGE SECRET!

ARIOL! I... I L--
?

BOOHOOHOO!
?
?
?

Come, come, BIZZBILLA, what's wrong with you?
BWAAAH!
Hoho!
Whoa!
Heheh
Bzzt Bzzt
Hoohoohoo!
Ho
Blabla

QUIET IN THE CLASS! Here, BIZZBILLA, blow your nose.
HONK

LATER...

Well? Has BIZZBILLA settled down?

No. Mrs. LATIFA said we had to send her back home because she had an eruption.

END

ARiOL
The Videogame
What are you up to, ARIOL? Have you fallen down the toilet?
NOK NOK

I'm almost done.

I hear the music from your thingamajig! I've told you a hundred times not to play in the bathroom! Come out, I have to pee!
Wait, I'm almost done.

I'm going to get mad, ARIOL!
Okay, okay, coming!

If I catch you fiddling around again in the bathroom with that thing, I'll take it away!
Well, you read in there!

Did you wash your hands, ARIOL?
No.

ARIOL, when you come out of the bathroom, you must wash your hands. How many years will I have to keep telling you?
But I didn't go!

What do you mean you didn't go? You sit in the bathroom for an hour and don't do anything?
Yes, I'm playing.

Are you constipated right now? If you're constipated, I'll cook you some prunes.
No, I'm okay.

So just what is that game? Show me.
Let's see.
It's my twiddler.

AAAH! Why there's our friend THUNDER HORSE! I recognize him!
Don't distract me.

Goodness he sure can make some leaps!
Don't jostle me! That's to avoid the flying roaches.
The little gray balls coming down there?

And you advance by pressing here?
No. Here, I jump. There, I advance or go back. But don't touch, please!

Jeez! There, that's it! You made me miss!
Let me give it a try.
TUT TUT

That's my TWIDDLER! You've no right taking it from me!
I'm not taking it from you, I'm borrowing it from you.

If you want one, buy one for yourself!
Hey, it sure seems to me I was the one who paid for it!
Yeah, but you gave it to me! Giving is giving, taking back is stealing!

ARIOL, where are you on your homework for tomorrow?
Mom! Dad's taking my TWIDDLER from me!

Answer me, have you finished your homework?
Uh... practically.
Go do your homework, ARIOL.

And you, give me that!
HEY!?
My TWIDDLER!

While I'm fixing dinner, you'll do me the pleasure of looking over your son's work.
Okay, okay...
My TWIDDLER!

Mister BLUNT told me his homework wasn't so brilliant lately!
Is that true, ARIOL?
Give me back my TWIDDLER!

Okay, get to work! Come into your room!
I'm disgusted!

Get your notebooks out. Show me what's to be done.
GRRRMBL GRROMMLL
History Road
THUNDER HORSE

"HISTORY ROAD." Funny name!
Mister BLUNT's the one who wants us to do this. We glue sheets of Bristol board to each other, and when you unfold it, it makes a road.
I see.
THUNDER HORSE

And what's on this road?
Well, here, for example, is pre-history. So we write down things and glue documents on.
Very good.
THUNDER HORSE

Tell me a little about pre-
history then. Prehistoric donkeys.
Tell me how they lived.
Uh...
THUNDER HORSE

They lived... on four legs.
Yes.
They'd eat
thistles.
Yes. And
where did
they live?
In caves.
Perfect.

And on the walls of those caves,
what did they do for decorations?
Shelves?
THUNDER HORSE

No. Look; you have some there in the photo.
Oh, yes!
Drawings!
"Frescos,"
you say.
THUNDER HORSE

That's a horse there. Can you imagine? A THUNDER HORSE of yore! It's like he's jumping, just like in your game!
Except that, in my game, he jumps for real and there are flying roaches.

Come on, we'll go into my office. We'll look on the INTERBEAST if we can find other pics to glue to your road.
Okay.

LATER...
So, you see? Homework isn't so awful! We learned lots of things while having fun.
That's true.

You're going to have the nicest road in the class, and Mister BLUNT will compliment you.
Can I have my TWIDDLER back?

And now, let's go eat Mommy's yummy tart with prehistoric thistles! HAHAHA!

Hey, that's weird. The kitchen door is never locked, usually.
CLAC
CLAC
CLAC

MUMULE? Are you there? Is dinner ready?
I'm almost done.
END

ARiOL
Before Dinner
We're going to play outside, Granny.
Stay in the yard. The mussels will be ready soon.

We can't play right in front of the house, because Granny's growing some flowers.
That's dumb.

That's her mimosa. We'll have to watch out if we play soccer.
And the shed over there?

That's Grandpa's toolshed.
Show me.

Not bad... there are weapons.

Come this way, I'll show you something secret.
I got a watering-machine gun!

MOVE IT!
Wait, I'm making sure nobody's following us.
No, it's okay.

Look.
What the heck is that?

The tank. Grandpa's gas is inside.
Your granddad has gas in his yard?
Yes, but don't repeat it.

Wait, but he's super-rich then! How come he doesn't even have a pool?
To do what? The beach is right there.

He could at least trade in his old car.
Shut up now! It's nighttime. We're the THUNDER HORSE commando unit. We're guarding the gas.

Suddenly, there's the Emperor MORODAN and his army attacking us! They're at the gate over there!
I'll kill 'em!
RATATATAT!

That's it. All dead.
No, there's some left! I'll throw a grenade at 'em.

DARN! The mimosa!
HAHA! Smack into it!

Come on! There's too many. We fall back towards the shed!
Yeah, I'm covering you. RATATATAT!

AAAH! ARIOL! I'm hit!
Don't move. I'm coming!

I'M GETTING THE WHEELBARROW TO TRANSPORT YOU!
Stop!

Well, what are you doing there? Are you wounded or not?
It's REX trying to lick my snout.
ARF! ARF!

REX! DOWN! LEAVE US ALONE!
YAP! YAPYAP!
BIENG!
BLANG!

He's getting in the wheelbarrow, that idiot!
Yeah, he always does that.
CLANG CLANG

Hey, help me, we'll push him down the incline.
Good idea.

THUNDER HORSE...
Avenger of the staaaaars...
YAP! YAP!

BAM! Into the manure!
AIRK!
PLOP

WE WON!
ARF ARF ARF!
HAHAHA! Look at REX's expression!

Star of the snows... my besotted heart...
Grandpa's watering. Want to go see him?
It's full of wasps here.

...was snared by your big eyes...
HEY, GRANDPA! CAN WE HELP YOU?

If you like. Go get the watering can and water Granny's flowers around the house.
Right away!

So, my boy? Are you having fun here with your buddy ARIOL?
Are you happy?
Yeah.

You see, the little trees I'm watering are pear trees. In the fall, we'll have some nice pears. Granny Annette will make some preserves. Do you like preserves?
Yeah.

ARIOL showed me your oil well.
And the yellow flowers here are called St. John's wort.

If I had oil like you, I'd have a gardener to water in my place.
What are you saying?

DINNER!
Ah! The grub's ready!
Turn off the spigot to the hose, please.

AAH! Granny ANNETTE's yummy, steamy mussels!

Serve yourselves. I have to take my meds for my circulation.

I want a mountain of them!

END

WATCH OUT FOR PAPERCUTZ

Welcome to the third tender-hearted ARIOL graphic novel by the awesomely talented team of Emmanuel Guibert and Marc Boutavant from Papercutz, those anthropomorphic creatures dedicated to publishing great graphic novels for all ages. I'm Jim Salamander, er, I mean, Jim Salicrup, your bleary-eyed Editor-in-Chief and President of the Giddy fan Club, here to enlighten you about another Papercutz series (or two)!

First, though, we want to mention how happy we are that ARIOL has seemed to find an audience so quickly in America. The first two volumes of ARIOL are already back to press for second printings, and that's great news for all ARIOL fans, as that means we get to keep publishing this wonderful series!

As I was looking over the stories for this volume, it struck me how focused it was on the simple joys of everyday life. We see ARIOL with his parents, his grandparents, his friends, and at school and at play. While many other Papercutz graphic novels also feature such scenes, ARIOL is all about that stuff, the other titles focus on mysteries or far-out adventures and include everyday elements as a bonus. We'll see, for example, Nancy Drew (in NANCY DREW AND THE CLUE CREW) spend time with her dad and Mrs. Gruen, her best friends Bess and George, and even see her at school, but Nancy is forever solving mysteries! Even Garfield (in THE GARFIELD SHOW) spends time with friends and family, but still will wind up battling lasagna-like aliens from Outer Space (we're not kidding)!

But there is another Papercutz series that does come very close to ARIOL, and also captures the magic of everyday family life. While in ARIOL, the characters all are animal-like creatures, in ERNEST & REBECCA, by Guillame Bianco and Antonello Dalena, Ernest is a magical microbe. But, that's not as big a deal as you might imagine, especially in ERNEST & REBECCA #3 "Grandpa Bug" and #4 "The Land of the Walking Stones." These graphic novels are also brilliantly written, and spectacularly drawn, and present awesome tales of everyday family life that will make you laugh and cry.

Essentially all I'm saying is, if you enjoy ARIOL, we suspect you'll also love ERNEST & REBECCA. But what do I know? After all, I'm just a donkey-- like you!

Thanks,

Jim

STAY IN TOUCH!

EMAIL: salicrup@papercutz.com
WEB: www.papercutz.com
TWITTER: @papercutzgn
FACEBOOK: PAPERCUTZGRAPHICNOVELS
REGULAR MAIL: Papercutz, 160 Broadway, Suite 700, East Wing, New York, NY 10038

Other Great Titles From PAPERCUTZ™